The Boss Babysitter

Adapted by Maggie Testa

Ready-to-Read

Simon Spotlight

New York   London   Toronto   Sydney   New Delhi

SIMON SPOTLIGHT
An imprint of Simon & Schuster Children's Publishing Division
1230 Avenue of the Americas, New York, New York 10020
This Simon Spotlight edition December 2019
DreamWorks The Boss Baby Back in Business © 2019 DreamWorks Animation LLC.
All Rights Reserved, including the right of reproduction in whole or in part in any form.
SIMON SPOTLIGHT, READY-TO-READ, and colophon are registered trademarks of
Simon & Schuster, Inc.
For information about special discounts for bulk purchases, please contact
Simon & Schuster Special Sales at 1-866-506-1949 or business@simonandschuster.com.
Manufactured in the United States of America 1019 LAK
10 9 8 7 6 5 4 3 2 1
ISBN 978-1-5344-5718-8 (hc)
ISBN 978-1-5344-5716-4 (pb)
ISBN 978-1-5344-5717-1 (eBook)

Mom and Dad are going out.
Tonight the babysitter
will be in charge.

"Who knows what rules she will have?" says Boss Baby. "She might not let you eat dessert."

"Down with babysitters!" the brothers chant.

The doorbell rings.

She is here!

"Are you ready for a super fun night?" Marisol asks.

"I am not feeling well," Tim says.
"Maybe you guys should stay home."

Marisol takes
his temperature.
Tim is not sick.

"You are in good hands," says Dad.

"See you later!"

"She is too good," says Tim.
"Then we will have to
make her look bad,"
says Boss Baby.

Boss Baby will
go to Baby Corp. to
see what he can learn
about Marisol.

Tim will stay at home
and try to find things
she is not good at.

Tim and Marisol

have so much fun!

When Boss Baby returns,
he tells Tim
what he found out
about Marisol.

There is nothing bad
about her!
It will be hard to fire her.
But Tim is not listening.
Tim likes Marisol!

Boss Baby does not
know what to do!
He needs his team to
help him.
Staci and Jimbo are
on the case.

Staci calls and pretends to be an angry mother. She makes Marisol believe she missed another babysitting job!

"We will be right over," says Marisol.

When they get to
the house, Boss Baby
sneaks away.

Tim catches Boss Baby.
"It is time to go home,"
says Tim.
But then he looks around.
Where are they?

"Why were you being mean to Marisol?" Tim asks.

"I did not want a babysitter," says Boss Baby.

"But I went too far."

Luckily, Marisol finds them and they all walk home.

But while they were out,
Staci and Jimbo
made a huge mess!
"What happened?"
asks Mom.
She is upset.

Marisol has a plan.
"A bat flew into the
house and did this!"
she tells them.
She has even planted a
fake bat to prove it.

Mom and Dad believe Marisol and tell her she can babysit again. Tim is happy Marisol will stay his babysitter. So is Boss Baby!